This Little Tiger book belongs to:

_____

_____

_____

Incy Wincy Spider

Keith Chapman

Jack Tickle

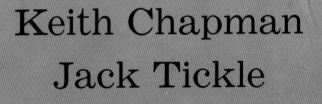

Little Tiger Press
LONDON

Whooo!

Incy Wincy Spider,
playing on a farm,
Spinning silver silk webs
high up in a barn.

From an open window
a gust of wind blows WHOOO!

whooOooosh

And Incy Wincy Spider
with a WHOOOOOSH goes too!

Incy Wincy Spider
is flying, there he goes!
He drifts on to a pink pig
and dangles from its nose.

OINKKK! grunts the pig
with Incy climbing up his snout.
And Incy Wincy Spider
is catapulted out!

Oinkkk!

Incy Wincy Spider,
he doesn't think it funny.
He's tangled on a grey goat
and calls out for his mummy.

B-E-H-H-H-H! bleats the goat,
who shakes from side to side.
And Incy Wincy Spider
begins another ride!

Behhhh!

Incy Wincy Spider,
can you see him now?
He's fluttered on to Buttercup,
the black and white young cow.

MOOOO! says Buttercup
and flicks her long, wide ears,
And Incy Wincy Spider
spins off and disappears!

MOOOO!

Incy Wincy Spider,
gliding through the air.
He hangs on to a duck's beak
and tickles under there.

QUACK! honks the yellow duck
and gives a great big sneeze.
And Incy Wincy Spider
floats off in the breeze!

QUACK!

Incy Wincy Spider,
what a dizzy day!
He's settled on a brown horse
chewing clumps of hay.

NE-

NEIGHHHH! snorts the horse
and jumps up really high.
And Incy Wincy Spider
pings off through the sky!

Shhhh!

Incy Wincy Spider
zooms past something red.
He shoots out lines of web silk
and sticks to cockerel's head.

COCK-A-DOODLE-DOO

The red and green
cockerel crows
COCK-A-DOODLE-DOO!
But Incy Wincy Spider,
where on earth are you?

Incy Wincy Spider,
what's he stuck on now?
A goat, horse or cockerel?
A pig, duck or cow?

No, he bounces with a

BOINNGGG!

Hooray! It's Mummy's web!
Now Incy Wincy Spider
is safely home in bed!

LITTLE TIGER PRESS
An imprint of Magi Publications
1 The Coda Centre, 189 Munster Road, London SW6 6AW
www.littletigerpress.com

First published in Great Britain 2005

This edition published 2005

Printed in China

4 6 8 10 9 7 5